THE
ICEMAN

THE ICEMAN

DON LESSEM

CROWN PUBLISHERS, INC.

New York

To Paula with love always

D.L.

Text copyright © 1994 by Don Lessem

Photographs: page 5 by Paul Hanny/Gamma Liaison; page 22 by Gerha Hinterleitner/Gamma Liaison; pages 14, 15, and 17 by Kenneth Garrett; pages 11,12, and 25 by Rex USA; pages 6-10, 18, and 20 by Sygma.

Illustrations on pages 21, 26-27, 29, and 30 copyright © by Bryn Barnard.
Illustrations on pages 13, 15, 23, and 24 by Marie Muscarnera.

Published by Crown Publishers, Inc., a Random House company, 201 East 50th Street, New York, New York 10022
CROWN is a trademark of Crown Publishers, Inc.
Manufactured in the United States of America

Library of Congress Cataloging-in-Publication Data
Lessem, Don.
The iceman / by Don Lessem.—1st ed.
p. cm.
Includes index.
1. Copper age—Italy—Trentino-Alto Adige—Juvenile literature.
2. Mummies—Italy—Trentino-Alto Adige—Juvenile literature.
3. Trentino-Alto Adige (Italy)—Antiquities—Juvenile literature.
4. Italy—Antiquities—Juvenile literature. [1. Man, Prehistoric.
2. Copper Age. 3. Excavations (Archaeology)] I. Title.
GN778.22.I8L47 1994
937'.3—dc20   93-31534
ISBN 0-517-59596-6 (trade)
0-517-59597-4 (lib. bdg.)

10 9 8 7 6 5 4 3 2 1
First Edition
Z0025639 3/96

On a sunny fall day in 1991, Erika and Helmut Simon were hiking in the mountains on the border between Austria and Italy. That afternoon the Simons roamed off the path and made a startling discovery: the small head and shoulders of a human body sticking out of the ice.

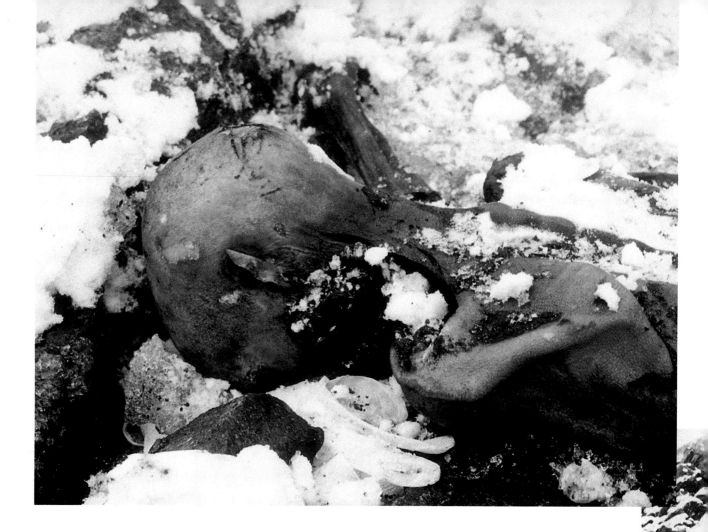

At first they thought the hairless figure was an abandoned doll. Then they noticed a small hole in the back of its skull. Perhaps this was a man who had been murdered, the Simons thought. They called the Italian police, who thought it might be the body of somebody killed in a recent hiking accident. The police left without attempting to dig the body out.

The Austrian police arrived by helicopter the next day. They tried—and failed—to remove the body from the thick ice with a jackhammer, tearing its clothes in the process. The police stopped digging when their jackhammer ran out of power and their helicopter was needed elsewhere. They decided to return the following week, with an expert on corpses to supervise them.

Meanwhile, news of the strange body spread quickly through

the mountains. Other officials and hikers arrived and tried to free it using axes and ski poles. Some took away items belonging to the body trapped in the ice. One unsuccessful rescuer even dug at the body with a stick that was found lying nearby. Later, the stick would prove to be a valuable part of the corpse's possessions.

The people who found the body had no idea how important their discovery was. A few days later, the police flew an Austrian scientist, Rainer Henn, to the site by helicopter to inspect the body. He noticed immediately that the corpse did not have the waxy skin of someone who had died recently. Instead, it looked yellowed and dried, like a mummy.

Dr. Henn could tell that this corpse was ancient, not modern, and for that reason it would be important to archaeologists, not the police. Archaeologists excavate their discoveries with great care to make sure nothing is overlooked, lost, or damaged. But Dr. Henn feared that the body would be further damaged by curious amateurs, so he decided to dig it out immediately and fly it to a laboratory. He had brought no tools with him, so he and his crew borrowed pickaxes and ski poles to finish the job of removing the body.

Dr. Henn wondered just how long this mummy had been preserved in the ice. Moments before the frozen body was loaded on the helicopter, a small stone knife with a wooden handle was discovered nearby. This was a primitive and very ancient tool—the first clue to the mummy's age.

More of the mummy's strange belongings were soon found, including clothes, a huge bow, and an ax. All of them would prove to be important clues to solving the mysteries of their owner's life and death. Even more important, the mummy and its possessions would turn out to give us our best view yet of the life of people in Europe thousands of years ago.

◀ ▲ Using crude tools, including pickaxes and ski poles, the recovery team led by Dr. Rainer Henn (*above left*) removes the Iceman from the glacier.

THE SCIENCE OF COLLECTING

The collecting of ancient human remains and belongings is part of the science of archaeology (ARE-key-OLL-uh-jee). Archaeologists excavate objects with great care to get all the information they can. They make a detailed map of the site and record all finds, however small. They often dig with small, specially designed tools to make sure nothing is missed or damaged.

The Iceman was not collected by archaeologists. Curious people came to the site before scientists and took some items. The mummy and its clothing were damaged because the body was removed in a hurry, without proper tools.

After scientists saw how valuable the discovery was, they returned to the site to make a more detailed search. People who had removed objects returned them. Though scientists were not the first ones at this important find, they have been able to gather a great deal of information from the Iceman and his possessions.

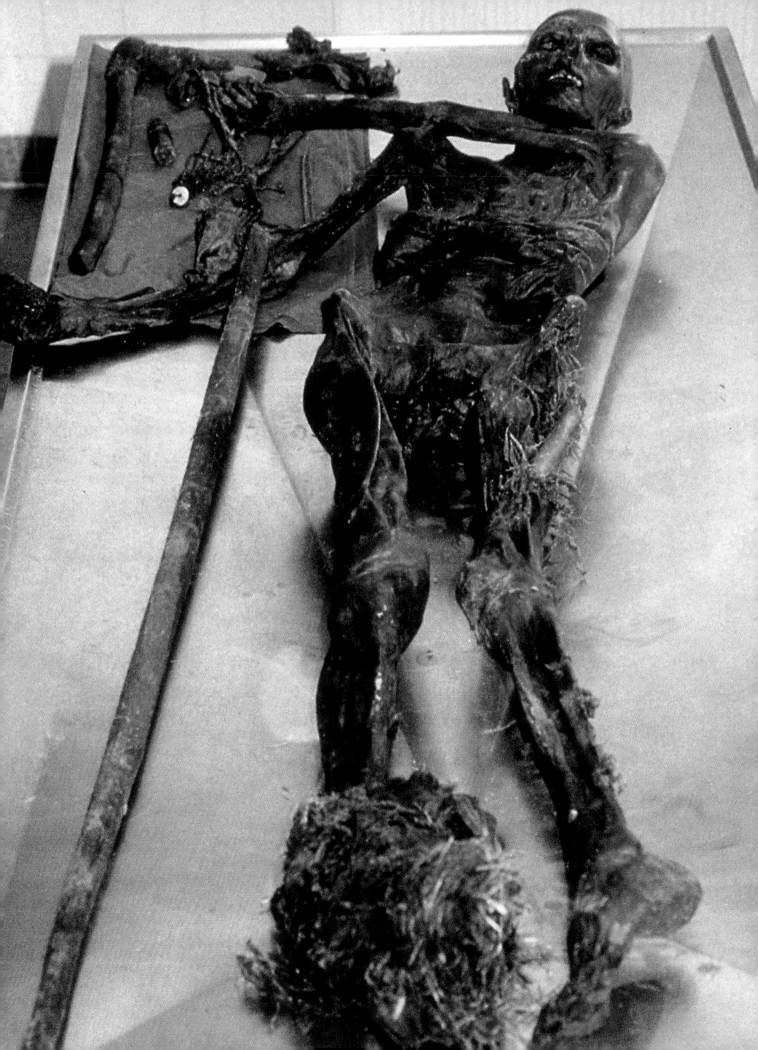

The mysterious body in the ice belonged to a man, soon nicknamed Ötzi (UTT-zee) by the local people, after the Ötztal, a valley near where he died. And they wondered, who was this man? Local children spoke of Ötzi as "the poor man who died alone in the snow."

Ötzi and his valuable belongings did not get proper scientific attention right away. He was flown to a village, then squeezed into a coffin for a ride to the city of Innsbruck. There Ötzi lay in a warm morgue for nearly a week, growing fungus, until an Austrian archaeologist, Dr. Konrad Spindler, was brought in to examine the corpse.

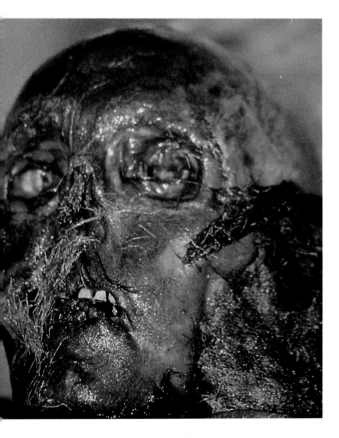

▲ A close-up view of Ötzi's mummified head shows how well his eyes were preserved. His nose and lips were disfigured—probably by the movement of the ice that covered him.

◀ Ötzi's body and belongings displayed on a table in Innsbruck. On his foot are remnants of a leather shoe stuffed with hay *(see page 20)*. Next to him are the tools and other objects that were found soon after his body was discovered, including a six-foot-long bow *(see pages 24-25)* and an ax *(see page 12)*.

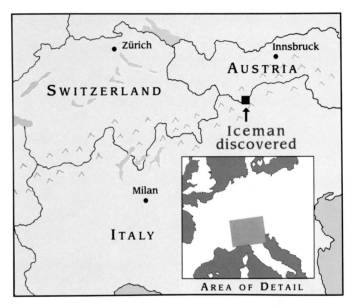

WHO KEEPS THE ICEMAN?

The Iceman was first thought to have been found in Austria. So he was excavated by the Austrian police and taken to a laboratory in Innsbruck, Austria, for study. Researchers then learned that he had died about 100 yards across the border, in Italy. As a result, Italian officials claimed that the body belonged to Italy and requested that it be returned to them. An international agreement arranged for the Iceman to go to Italy on September 19, 1994—three years from the day he was found.

Dr. Spindler immediately guessed that Ötzi could be as much as 4,000 years old—which would make him the oldest complete mummy ever found! It was not the Iceman himself but the ax that was found with him that led Dr. Spindler to estimate Ötzi's age. Ötzi's ax was an impressive weapon, with a wedge-shaped four-inch metal blade. The blade was wrapped with cow leather and glue from the gum of birch trees. It was held tightly in an L-shaped handle made of yew wood. Dr. Spindler guessed the blade of this well-made tool was fashioned from bronze, a metal that came into use 4,000 years ago. But laboratory studies showed that Dr. Spindler's guess was wrong—and that Ötzi was even older than he had thought. The ax blade was made of almost pure copper, a metal put into use by blacksmiths almost two thousand years before bronze. Ötzi was between 5,000 and 5,500 years old and belonged to the Copper Age.

▼ The flint-bladed knife that first alerted Ötzi's discoverers to his age (*see page 8*).

Ötzi's ax as it may have looked when he used it (*above*) and as it was found (*below*).

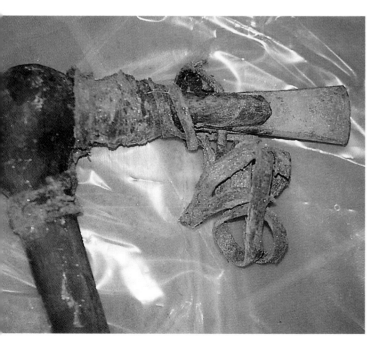

HOW OLD WAS THE ICEMAN?

It wasn't difficult to determine how old the Iceman was when he died. The condition of his bones and teeth, which show a full-grown healthy person, indicates that he was between the ages of 25 and 40.

Figuring out how long the Iceman has been a mummy was a harder problem. His tools are similar to those found at sites known to be more than 5,000 years old. And a method called *carbon dating* verified this. All living things, and many objects, contain the element carbon. Part of that carbon is in a form that decays at a steady rate. By measuring how much of this form of carbon has decayed, scientists can estimate the age of an animal, plant, or object. Carbon dating tells us that the Iceman is 5,000 to 5,500 years old.

13

▲ These wood-and-mud stilt houses were reconstructed at Lac de Chalain in eastern France by archaeologists using evidence from the remains of European Copper Age villages. Ötzi may have visited villages that looked something like this.

There are Copper Age villages spread across the middle of Europe, including several in Switzerland, not far north of where Ötzi was found. Research has shown that these villages consisted of wood-and-mud houses built on stilts along muddy lake shores. Villagers built wheeled carts and used plows for farming. They grew barley, peas, and flax for linen clothes, and they fished and hunted for food. They raised animals: dogs, sheep, goats, pigs, and cattle. And they made whole-grain bread from the barley they grew, and butter from milk. They traded with other peoples near and far away, bartering limestone jewelry they made with people from the south for parsley and peppermint.

▲ Ötzi may have seen wheels like this in use. Excavated in Zürich, Switzerland, this wheel is made of a solid piece of wood and dates back to 3200 B.C. It may be the oldest ever found. Next to it is a model showing what a Copper Age wagon might have looked like.

MAKING COPPER

Copper was the first metal used by prehistoric man. It was found in rocks, including those at the base of the mountains where the Iceman died. The drawing below shows how copper was made. Coppersmiths built underground fires into which they placed rocks containing copper. They blew into the fire pit through hollowed-out sticks. When the temperature neared 2,000°F, the copper melted and separated from the rock around it. The pure copper was shaped into bars, and then re-melted and poured into molds to make tools. Copper made far sharper, stronger tools than stone did.

Copper was first used in Europe about 6,000 years ago (4000 B.C.). The Copper Age lasted until about 4,200 years ago (2200 B.C.), when copper was replaced by bronze and the Bronze Age began.

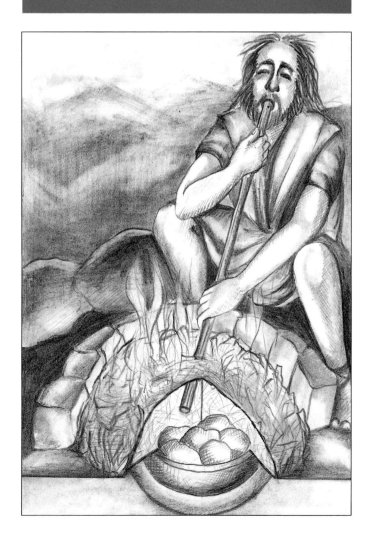

The remains of many Copper Age villages have been discovered and excavated, but it is Ötzi who has given archaeologists their best indication of what the people of Europe actually looked like 5,500 years ago. From his well-preserved mummy, we can tell a lot about the Iceman's appearance. He was short—about 5 feet 2 inches. But he was powerful, as the enormous bow that was found with him indicates. It was far larger than the Iceman himself and would have required great strength to draw back and fire arrows from.

Scientists are sure that Ötzi had curly brown hair. How do we know that when the hair on his body and head was not preserved? Hairs were discovered trapped in his clothes. The ends of those hairs were evenly snipped, indicating that somebody had given Ötzi a haircut.

TAKING CARE OF THE ICEMAN

To protect the Iceman, Dr. Spindler and his colleagues from the Institute for Prehistory and Early History in Innsbruck sprayed his body with a chemical to kill the mold that had been growing from the time the body was found. Then they placed the body in a freezer. There the temperature was kept at exactly 21°F and the humidity at 98 percent—just the icy conditions in which Ötzi had been preserved until he was found.

Ötzi remains on ice. He is never removed from his frozen container for more than 20 minutes at a time, and then only for scientific study. Meanwhile, the investigation of Ötzi and his belongings goes on, with scientists around the world studying pieces of his skin, bones, clothes, and tools.

▶ Using measurements and X rays of Ötzi's skull and studies of Europeans today, artist John Gurche made this model showing how Ötzi might have looked. The skin is made of soft plastic and tinted red to imitate Ötzi's windburned skin. The eyes are made of glass.

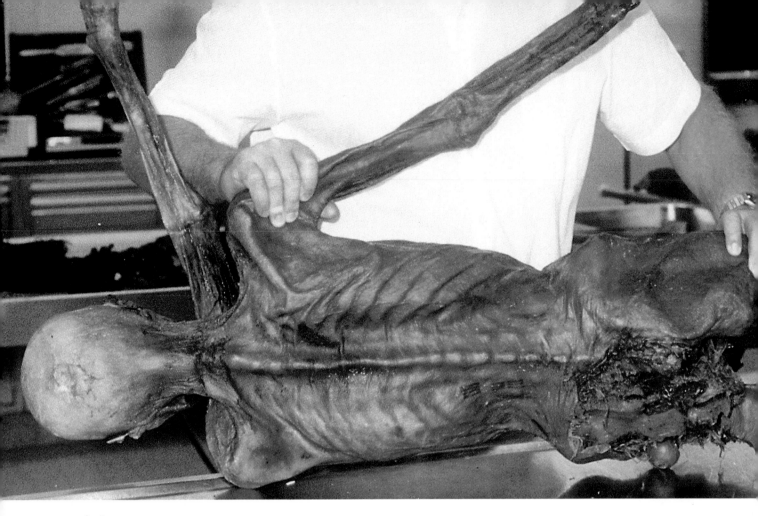

▲ Ötzi's back. In the lower part of the picture, near his spine, are three groups of tattooed lines.

Investigators discovered mysterious tattoos on Ötzi's body. Four stripes, each three inches long, ran across the top of his left foot. On his left kneecap he wore a cross. And three groups of small bars lined his lower back. These weren't decorations meant for others to see, for they appeared only on parts of his body that would have been hidden by his clothing. Maybe they were a badge of religious importance.

Ötzi may have made some of them himself, with a needle and ash or dye. But someone else had to make the tattoos on his back.

From Ötzi's teeth, scientists drew conclusions about what he ate. His diet seems to have been richest in bread, for his teeth were ground down, as they could only be from eating grains for many years.

From Ötzi's body, researchers have also figured out that he died of exposure to the cold. He probably encountered an unexpected wintry storm in fall. Without sufficient clothing to keep himself warm, or food to nourish him, his body temperature dropped until he died.

SNOW

GLACIAL ICE

↑
Position of body

ROCK

The Iceman's remarkable preservation and his discovery occurred only because of a series of lucky events.

Many people die on icy mountains. If their bodies are not found, glaciers eventually crush them. But the Iceman died in a hollow that glaciers never reached. Light snow covered his body soon after he died and kept it from decay as it dried out. Then the snow was covered with thick layers of ice, which built up to form a glacier. Because it was in a hollow, the Iceman's body was not crushed by the ice; instead, the ice passed over him (*left*).

In the last 70 years the weather has turned warmer, and as a result, the glaciers in the Alps have retreated. In the spring of 1991, a storm in the Sahara Desert sent clouds of dust into the air, which settled on the snow-covered mountains where the Iceman was buried. The dark dust absorbed the heat of the sun instead of reflecting it, as white snow would have. Combined with a warm summer, it helped melt the snow and ice quickly. The Iceman emerged for the first time in 5,000 years. Then, within days, his body was discovered—before the air could destroy it or snow cover it over again.

But why didn't Ötzi have the strength to walk down the mountain? Perhaps the storm was too fierce. Maybe he was weak from illness, though scientists have yet to find any evidence that he was sick.

It is possible that Ötzi was suffering from a broken arm. His left arm is cracked. This injury may have been caused by his rough removal from the ice. But the skin on his arm is undamaged, suggesting that it was broken while he was still alive. Perhaps the pain of a broken arm, injured in a mountain fall, weakened this strong man.

Much of Ötzi's clothing was destroyed during the rough and sloppy excavation. But from many scraps found with the body, scientists have determined that he wore leather pants and a long-sleeved jacket made of deer, goat, and ibex hide, with the fur side turned out. The pieces of hide had been skillfully stitched together with threads made of animal sinews and grass. Rough repairs had also been made—probably by Ötzi himself—using grass thread.

He also wore a huge cape, braided from strands of grass. This heavy poncho resembled a Hawaiian grass skirt, except that it was tied around the neck, not the waist. A piece of fur discovered near Ötzi may have been a fur cap.

On Ötzi's feet were shoes—soft ovals, size six, made of leather and filled with a warm stuffing of hay. Grass laces, kept dry by a leather flap, were strung through eyeholes to keep his feet snug.

Ötzi may have worn jewelry. Near his body lay a leather string with a fringe, strung through a two-inch disk made of white stone. This mysterious object may have been Ötzi's necklace.

▲ Ötzi's "necklace"—a white stone disk on a leather string.

▶ One of Ötzi's grass-stuffed shoes.

▲ Ötzi as he may have looked dressed in his hat, his braided-grass cape, his shoes, and his necklace. With him are some of the things he carried: his ax, his bow and quiver of arrows, his knife, his backpack, and his birch-bark container, which may have contained tinder for starting fires.

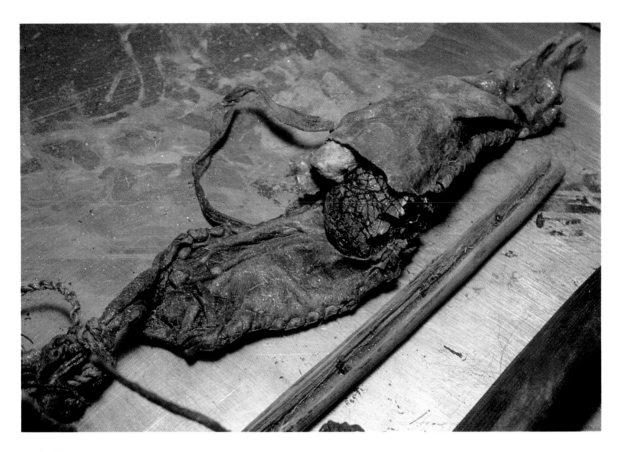

▲ Ötzi's leather pouch, which he probably wore like a modern fanny pack.

Ötzi wasn't traveling light. In addition to his heavy cape, he was hauling a wood-frame backpack. It was a piece of this backpack that one of Ötzi's rescuers had used to try to dig him out of the ice.

Scientists can't tell what Ötzi carried in the backpack. But a soft leather pouch, like a modern fanny pack, was also found, with its contents intact. There were two pieces of flint, which could have been used for making tools and for striking sparks to start fires. There was also a four-inch-long wooden stick, like a fat pencil, with a tip made of deer antler. Ötzi may have used this tool for sharpening the chunks of flint. The pack also contained grass string and a needle-pointed awl made from a thin shaft of bone.

Near Ötzi's body, researchers found a frozen sloeberry and a slice of antelope meat, which he might have been carrying as a snack, and two mushrooms strung on a piece of leather. Scientists know that this kind of mushroom can be used to fight sickness; perhaps Ötzi was carrying them as medicine. Ötzi also carried two strips of felt and a small container made of birch bark. Scientists think he may have used the felt as tinder for starting fires and the birch-bark container to carry the felt in.

For cutting up leather or small animals, the Iceman carried a tiny knife with a flint blade the size of his thumb and a handle of ash wood. He protected this tool with a sheath woven of grass.

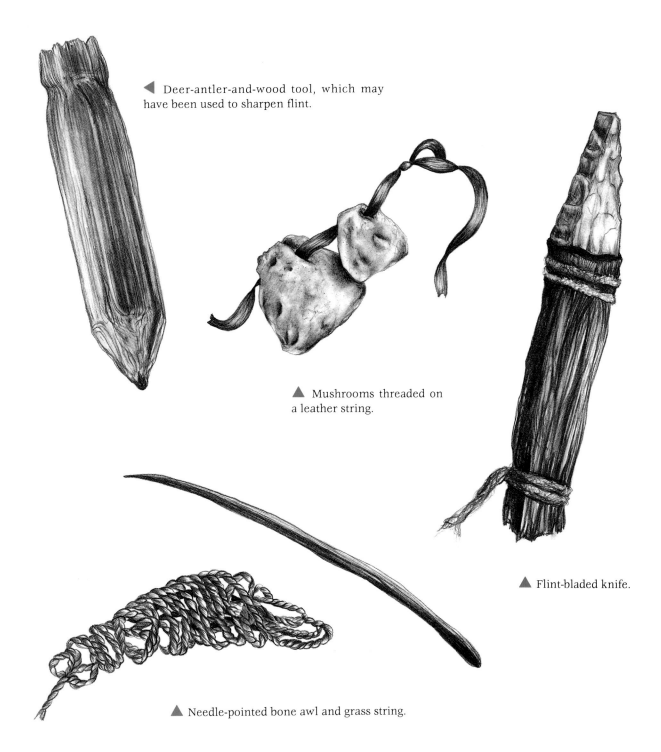

◄ Deer-antler-and-wood tool, which may have been used to sharpen flint.

▲ Mushrooms threaded on a leather string.

▲ Flint-bladed knife.

▲ Needle-pointed bone awl and grass string.

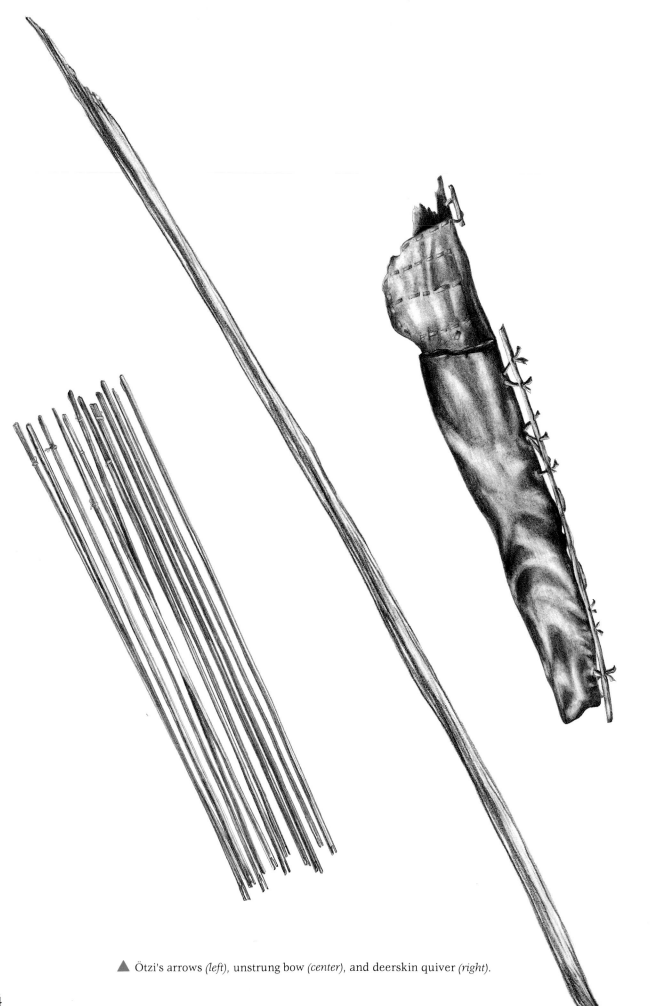

▲ Ötzi's arrows *(left)*, unstrung bow *(center)*, and deerskin quiver *(right)*.

▲ Ötzi's arrows. Two of them have tail feathers in place.

After his copper-bladed ax, the most impressive of Ötzi's possessions were his bow and arrows. The bow was nearly six feet long and made of yew, the best wood available for making bows. Ötzi's bow was new. It had not yet been notched or strung, and fresh cut marks from an ax still show on its surface.

Ötzi carried his arrows in a deerskin quiver, which also held a ball of grass string, a piece of deer antler, and a few unshaped flints. In all, there were a dozen shafts of viburnum wood for arrows Ötzi hadn't finished making.

But two arrows were complete and very well crafted. Flint, chipped perfectly into an arrowhead, had been attached to each shaft with gum made from the boiled roots of birch trees. With this glue, feathers were set at angles on the ends of the shaft to make the arrow spin and so travel straight in flight.

▲ This artist's impression of Ötzi's arrival at a lakeside village is based on what is known about daily life in the Copper Age. In the background is the mountainous terrain of the Alps. Houses built of wood and mud stand on stilts at the edge of a lake. Nearby are cultivated fields and a primitive wagon. On the lake a person is fishing from a boat.

Ötzi and the everyday objects that were found beside him are unique and wonderfully preserved clues to daily life in a time that has long been mysterious. With their help, we can imagine what life might have been like in the Copper Age and how Ötzi lived and died. We can never be certain, but it may have been something like this:

Ötzi may have been a shepherd herding sheep, a trader trading stone and metal for tools, or even a medicine man in search of messages from gods. Whatever the reason, Ötzi had hiked high into the mountains. He was strong and well equipped, perhaps a leader among his people. The tattoo lines on his knee, foot, and back may have been religious emblems or a sign of his bravery or status.

Ötzi was a welcome visitor to the villages along his route. If he was a shepherd, he would have brought the villagers meat (since wool was not yet used for clothing). If he was a trader, he would have brought them flint for tools or copper for weapons.

Ötzi may have admired the villagers' talents. They used wheeled wagons and plows to farm. They sewed linen clothes and shoes expertly. They fed him butter and other delicacies.

The villagers may have been impressed with the hard flints Ötzi had brought—wonderful stones for making daggers and knives—and with his fine ax. But Ötzi would not part with the ax. He had traveled far to the south and traded away many of his belongings to the copper workers for his ax.

Ötzi was handy and so found many uses for his ax. He had been wielding it lately to make a new bow to replace the one he'd traded away or broken. It was a huge bow, taller than he was. It took all his strength to pull the bowstring.

Ötzi had been hunting since he was a child. He had learned to feather his arrows at an angle to make them spin in flight and hold their course. After crossing the mountains, Ötzi planned to finish his new bow and arrows. Then he could hunt in the woods for ibex, deer, and boar, and kill threatening bears and wolves. But for now, his mind was on traveling across the treeless high mountains in the thin, cold air.

In the soft deerskin suit and grass cape made for him by the village tailors, Ötzi was dressed for chill mountain weather. He had stuffed his shoes with mountain grass to protect his feet from the cold. He wore a fur cap on his head.

But the autumn air turned even colder than Ötzi had expected. He huddled in the shelter of a rock hollow. He was too cold and tired to eat the last of the antelope meat and berries he had brought with him.

Ötzi tried to start a fire. He had flint to strike a spark and strips of felt to help the fire along. But far above the tree line, Ötzi could find no branches to keep a fire going. Perhaps falling snow snuffed out the few sparks he had created.

Ötzi's only hope for survival was to move on through the mountain pass and down into the valley. But he was too weak to move. Maybe he was sick or injured.

Ötzi carefully laid his belongings, including his beautiful ax, against the rocks around him. He lay down to sleep on his left side atop a large stone as the snow fell through the frigid air.

Days later, when Ötzi did not appear, other shepherds, or friends from the village, may have come looking for him. If they came upon the spot where he lay down, they would have found only a blanket of snow.

In cold isolation, Ötzi had quietly died. Five thousand years later, his snow blanket was finally removed. At last Ötzi was found, along with his treasures. Their value is beyond measure, for they give us our best view yet of the lost world of our Copper Age ancestors.

I N D E X

A B O U T   T H E   A U T H O R

Don Lessem's books include *Digging Up Tyrannosaurus Rex* (with John R. Horner), an NSTA/CBC Outstanding Science Trade Book for Children, and for adults *The Complete T. Rex* and *Kings of Creation*, a survey of dinosaur discoveries around the world. He has reported on science topics for the *Boston Globe*, the *New York Times, Life*, and many other publications and has written and hosted documentaries for the PBS television series *NOVA*. Mr. Lessem is also the founder of the Dinosaur Society, a nonprofit organization created to benefit dinosaur science. He lives in Waban, Massachusetts.